☆☆☆ ARLO & PIPS ☆☆☆

JOIN THE CROW CROWD!

ELISE GRAVEL

An Imprint of HarperCollins*Publishers*

HarperAlley is an imprint of HarperCollins Publishers.

Arlo & Pips #2: Join the Crow Crowd!
Copyright © 2021 by Elise Gravel
All rights reserved. Printed in Bosnia and Herzegovina.
No part of this book may be used or reproduced in any manner whatsoever without written permission except in the case
of brief quotations embodied in critical articles and reviews. For information address HarperCollins Children's Books, a
division of HarperCollins Publishers, 195 Broadway, New York, NY 10007.

www.harperalley.com

Library of Congress Control Number: 2020950523
ISBN 978-0-06-239423-1 (trade bdg.) — ISBN 978-0-06-305077-8 (pbk.)

The artist used Photoshop to create the digital illustrations for this book.
Typography by Elise Gravel and Chrisila Maida
21 22 23 24 25   GPS   10 9 8 7 6 5 4 3 2 1

❖
First Edition

To Andrew Arnold

4

5

Well, let's find you something better to do.

Hmm . . . How about treasure hunting?

Nah . . . I have enough treasures.

ENOUGH TREASURES?

Well, you've got me.

I know, Pips, and you're such a great friend.

But crows have to hang out with other crows.

Crows are social birds, and they often live in groups.

14

Crows can hold a grudge for a very long time.

16

A MURDER?

What are you talking about?

"Murder" is what humans call a group of crows.

 That's true! Weird, huh?

But . . . why?

No idea.

I think humans find us scary for some reason.

In certain cultures, crows are known as "tricksters." Others believe they bring bad luck or are a bad omen.

Go talk to them!

I'm shy. There are too many of them.

Start with one! Like that girl over there.

Can you talk to her first?

She speaks funny!

It's not funny— she just has a different accent! I like it.

Hello, Marla! Noice to meet you, too!

 Just like humans, crows from different groups have different accents and they adapt to "fit in"!

Humans waste 1.3 billion tons of food every year. I can't believe it, either.

28

29

Thanks!

Hmm.

My beak is too big. It can't reach the water.

Let me help you.

This rock will do.

?

PLOP!

Crows do that!

34

Oh, humans gave me that. It's to identify me.

I used to be a lab crow. Some humans wanted to study me.

What's a lab?

It's a place where humans do experiments. They wanted to know how my brain works.

Crows are so smart that scientists love to observe and study them.

Crows are very curious; they always want to learn. That's how they get so smart.

39

Ornithologists are scientists who study birds.

Crows love to play! I've seen videos of crows snowboarding on slanted roofs, playing on a seesaw. . . . And bird species that like to play are very rare!

What kinds of games?

Mostly puzzles.

Some of those puzzles were so hard.

We also played tic-tac-toe.

And she taught me some circus tricks, just for fun.

 Crows have solved very complex puzzles that even monkeys couldn't figure out!

She also taught me a bunch of human words.

Like what?

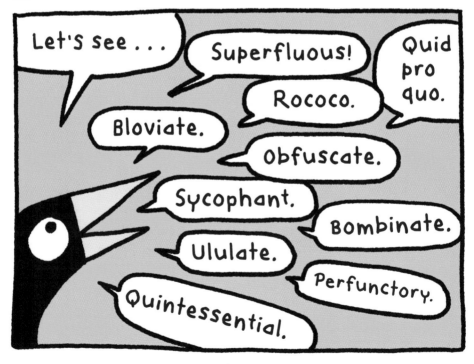

Let's see . . .

Superfluous!

Quid pro quo.

Rococo.

Bloviate.

Obfuscate.

Sycophant.

Bombinate.

Ululate.

Perfunctory.

Quintessential.

Whoa! Those are fancy words.

When I got better, Ani set me free.

She was a good human. I liked her, and I still visit her sometimes. ⭐

 Crows remember humans who were nice to them. So ... be nice to them!

FLOP!

What are you doing?

Marla is so SMART.

Smarter than ME, even.

What do people do when they're in love?

I don't know, Arlo. You're the smart one.

Love is making my brain all sluggish. I can't think.

Maybe I should tell her how amazing I am?

How handsome, how clever, how muscular, how funny, how . . .

Arlo.

That's a BAD idea. Nobody likes show-offs.

But I'm the best show-off of all time!

That's for sure.

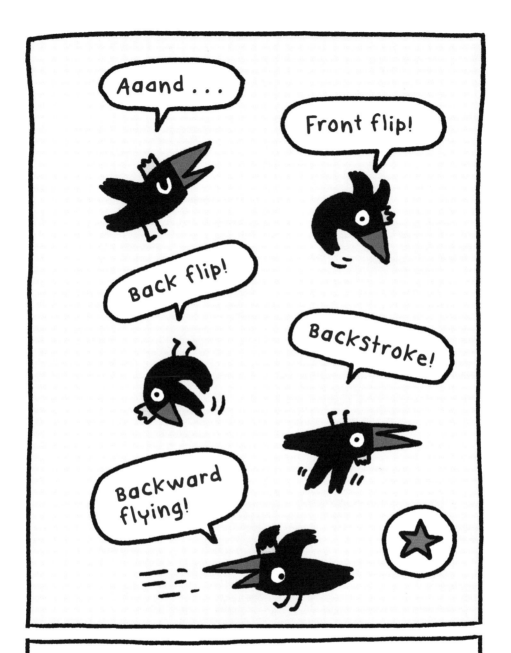

Crows are amazing acrobats, and enjoy doing tricks.

54

I'll go look through my collection!

I'll come with you.

Whoa. It got bigger since the last time I saw it!

Now, let's see . . . what should I give her?

A button? Boring. An earring? Not original. A painted toenail? Nah.

Crows can't read, either.